THE FIREWORKS SHOW

Written by Joanne Meier and Cecilia Minden • Illustrated by Bob Ostrom
Created by Herbie J. Thorpe

ABOUT THE AUTHORS

Joanne Meier, PhD, has worked as an elementary school teacher, university professor, and researcher. She earned her BA in early childhood education from the University of South Carolina, and her MEd and PhD in education from the University of Virginia. She currently works as a literacy consultant for schools and private organizations. Joanne lives in Virginia with her husband Eric, daughters Kella and Erin, two cats, and a gerbil.

Cecilia Minden, PhD, is the former director of the Language and Literacy Program at the Harvard Graduate School of Education. She is now a reading consultant for school and library publications. She earned her PhD in reading education from the University of Virginia. Cecilia and her husband, Dave Cupp, live outside Chapel Hill, North Carolina. They enjoy sharing their love of reading with their grandchildren, Chelsea and Qadir.

ABOUT THE ILLUSTRATOR

Bob Ostrom has been illustrating children's books for nearly twenty years. A graduate of the New England School of Art & Design at Suffolk University, Bob has worked for such companies as Disney, Nickelodeon, and Cartoon Network. He lives in North Carolina with his wife Melissa and three children, Will, Charlie, and Mae.

ABOUT THE SERIES CREATOR

Herbie J. Thorpe had long envisioned a beginning-readers' series about a fun, energetic bear with a big imagination. Herbie is a book lover and an avid supporter of libraries and the role they play in fostering the love of reading. He consults with librarians and matches them with the perfect books for their students and patrons. He lives in Louisiana with his wife Misty and their daughter Carson.

The Child's World

Published in the United States of America by The Child's World®
1980 Lookout Drive • Mankato, MN 56003-1705
800-599-READ • www.childsworld.com

Acknowledgments
The Child's World®: Mary Berendes, Publishing Director
The Design Lab: Kathleen Petelinsek, Design
Artistic Assistant: Richard Carbajal

Library of Congress Cataloging-in-Publication Data
Meier, Joanne D.
  The fireworks show / by Joanne Meier and Cecilia Minden;
illustrated by Bob Ostrom.
    p. cm. — (Herbster readers)
  ISBN 978-1-60253-216-8 (library bound : alk. paper)
  [1. Fireworks—Fiction. 2. Bears—Fiction.] I. Minden, Cecilia.
II. Ostrom, Bob, ill. III. Title. IV. Series.

PZ7.M5148Fjf 2009
[E]—dc22   2009003978

Herbie Bear's family was at the lake.

They were visiting Pappy and Nana.

It was the Fourth of July.

"I love fireworks!" said Herbie.

6

"Me too," said Nana.

7

"I heard there are special fireworks this year," said Nana.

"They are ones we've never seen before."

10

Everyone got on the boat.

"Do we have everything?" asked Pappy.

Pappy turned on the motor and lights.

They headed away from the dock.

13

Many boats were out on the lake.

Everyone waited for dark.

The sun went down.

"It's almost time!" shouted Hank.

The fireworks started. **BANG!**

They exploded in the sky.

"I see red, white, and blue!" said Hannah.

"The colors fill the sky!"

22

Herbie sat up front. Swimming all day had made him sleepy.

The fireworks looked like letters to Herbie.

"That looks like an H," he said to himself.

"That looks like an E," he said.

"And there's an R!"

"The fireworks are spelling my name!"
said Herbie. "How cool!"

"Wake up, Herbie," said Pappy.

"You'll miss the big ending."

Herbie rubbed his eyes and smiled.